This edition published by Parragon in 2013
Parragon
Chartist House
15–17 Trim Street
Bath BA1 1HA, UK
www.parragon.com

ISBN 978-1-78186-636-8

Printed in China

Peter Pan

PaRRagon

Bath • New York • Singapore • Hong Kong • Cologne • Delhi
Melbourne • Amsterdam • Johannesburg • Shenzhen

There once was a house in London where the Darling family lived. There were Mr and Mrs Darling and their three children, Wendy, John and Michael.

Watching over the children was Nana, the nursemaid, who also happened to be a dog.

This was the home that Peter Pan often visited.

He chose this house for one very special reason: there were people there who believed in him. Wendy would tell stories of Peter Pan and his adventures in a magical place called Never Land. Peter loved to sit in the shadows and listen.

One night, while the Darling children were sleeping, Peter Pan and his fairy friend, Tinker Bell, slipped into the nursery. Peter had left his shadow behind the last time he visited. He'd come back to find it.

Suddenly, Wendy woke up. "Peter Pan!" she cried. "I knew you'd come back!" She had been keeping his shadow safe.

Carefully, she sewed Peter's shadow back onto his feet.

Wendy explained to Peter that tonight was her last night in the nursery. "I have to grow up tomorrow," she said.

"I won't have it!" Peter cried. "Come on! We're going to Never Land. You'll never grow up there!"

Wendy woke John and Michael so that they could come too. "But Peter," said Wendy. "How do we get there?"

"Fly, of course!" answered Peter. He sprinkled the children with Tinker Bell's pixie dust and told them to think happy thoughts. Soon they were flying out of the window!

Peter, Tink and the children soared through the skies
and finally spotted Never Land down below.

"There's a pirate ship!" cried Michael.

The captain of the pirate ship was Peter's greatest
enemy – Captain Hook!

"Blast that Peter Pan!" said Hook as he studied a map of Never Land. "If I could only find his hideout, I'd trap him."

Captain Hook got his name because he had a hook where his hand should have been. A crocodile had bitten it off long ago, and was still after the rest of him!

Luckily for Hook, there was an alarm clock in the crocodile's belly that went 'tick-tock, tick-tock', so Hook could hear him coming.

Meanwhile, Peter Pan had taken Wendy to see
the Mermaid Lagoon. But John and Michael had no
interest in mermaids. They wanted an adventure with
Peter's friends, the Lost Boys!

"John, you be the leader," cried the Lost Boys.
Then, lining up behind him, they marched off into
the forest. As they marched along, the Lost Boys and
John made a plan. They would be very clever and
capture the Indians!

The plan might have worked, too, if the Indians hadn't caught them first! Michael and John were frightened until the Lost Boys explained that it was just a game – the Indians always let them go.

But this time the Chief wouldn't set them free. He thought that they had kidnapped his daughter, Tiger Lily!

Nearby, Peter was showing Wendy the Mermaid
Lagoon. Suddenly he spotted Hook and Smee rowing
by in a small boat. Tied up in the back was Tiger Lily.

"It looks like they're headed for Skull Rock," Peter
said. "Let's see what they're up to."

Sure enough, Hook was holding Tiger Lily prisoner!
He had tied her to a rock in the sea and was asking
her about Peter Pan's hideout. Hook thought she
could tell him where it was.

Peter set off to rescue Tiger Lily before the tide
came in.

Peter Pan drew his sword and fought Captain Hook back and forth. Wendy could barely watch.

"I've got you this time, Pan!" cried Captain Hook, forcing Peter near to the edge of a cliff. But Peter danced out of the way, into thin air!

Suddenly, Captain Hook tumbled off the cliff. Smee picked him up in the row boat, and the crocodile started to chase them!

While they rowed away, Peter rescued Tiger Lily.

The Indian Chief was so pleased to get his
daughter back that he gave Peter a headdress
and proclaimed him 'Chief Little Flying Eagle'.

But not everyone joined in the celebrations. Back onboard his pirate ship, Captain Hook was hatching an evil plot to get rid of Peter Pan.

Hook had lured jealous Tinker Bell into his lair and promised that he would get rid of Wendy, if she would tell him where Peter's hideout was. But as soon as Tink told him, he locked her in a glass lantern!

Meanwhile at Peter's hideout, Wendy knew that she and her brothers must go home soon. She sang about the wonders of a real mother until even the Lost Boys wanted to go to London! Only Peter wanted to stay.

One by one, the Lost Boys, Wendy, John and Michael left the hideout – only to walk right into the arms of waiting pirates!

Captain Hook and his pirate gang led the prisoners away and tied them to the mast of his ship.

"I have left a little present for Peter," Captain Hook told Smee. "It is due to blast off at six o'clock."

From her glass cage, Tinker Bell overheard Hook's plan. She was furious! She knocked over the lantern and, with a CRACK, she was free.

Tinker Bell reached Peter's hideout just in time –
he was about to open the package! She tried to pull
the package away, there was no time to explain.

But it was too late. The box began to smoke.
Suddenly – KABOOM!

The explosion was so huge that it rocked Hook's ship! Captain Hook smiled.

"Join me, or walk the plank," Hook shouted.

"Join you? Never!" cried Wendy. She walked to the end of the plank and jumped. But there was no splash....

Peter Pan had flown to save Wendy! He set her down safely, then flew up onto the rigging. Hook scrambled up after him and drew his sword.

As Peter and Hook clashed swords, Wendy, Michael, John and the Lost Boys battled it out with the other pirates.

Suddenly, Captain Hook lost his balance. He fell overboard and into the water, where a familiar crocodile was waiting....

"Hooray for Captain Pan!" cried all the children.

"All right, ya swabs," said Peter. "We're castin' off for London."

"Michael, John, we're going home!" smiled Wendy.

"Hoist the anchor!" cried Peter. "Tink, let's have some of your pixie dust!"

Tinker Bell flew around the ship, sprinkling her magical dust as she went. Then, up, up, up went the ship, and as it rose, it began to glow like gold.

Back in London, Mrs Darling found Wendy asleep by
the window.

"Oh, Mother, we're back!" cried Wendy. She told her
parents all about their wonderful adventure in Never Land.

"I'm going to bed," announced Mr Darling. But as he
turned to leave, he noticed, passing in front of the moon,
a ship made of clouds....

"You know," said Mr Darling, "I have the strangest
feeling I've seen that ship before. A long, long time ago,
when I was very young."

And, indeed, he had.